# Long Live King Bob!

By Lucy Rosen

Little, Brown and Company

Hachette Book Group
1290 Avenue of the Americas, New York, NY 10104
Visit us at lb-kids.com

LB kids is an imprint of Little, Brown and Company.
The LB kids name and logo are trademarks of
Hachette Book Group, Inc.

The publisher is not responsible for websites
(or their content) that are not owned by the publisher.

First Edition: May 2015

ISBN 978-0-316-29993-0

10 9 8 7 6 5 4 3 2 1

CW

Printed in the United States of America

minionsmovie.com

Stuart, Bob, and Kevin are Minions on a mission. They're looking for the world's biggest, baddest villain to serve. (Minions live to help bad guys. It's kind of their thing.)

At long last, after many years of searching, the Minions find the perfect master: Scarlet Overkill, the most famous criminal mastermind of her generation!

Scarlet brings the Minions to her castle in London, England. She shows them a picture of Queen Elizabeth, points to the crown atop the queen's head, and says, "Steal me the crown, and all your dreams come true!" The Minions are excited about their mission. Scarlet sends them to Herb's lab to pick up some supplies for the heist.

Herb is Scarlet's husband. He is also an evil inventor. "So you're here for gear!" he says as they enter his lab.

"Bob, Robert, Bobby, my boy—you get my far-out Stretch Suit," Herb says. "Kevin, Kev-Bo, Seventh Kevin. You are the proud owner of my Lava-Lamp Gun! And finally, Stu. Stu-art, Stuperman, Beef Stu. I got you the coolest invention, probably ever. Hypno-Hat!"

The Minions gear up. They are ready to go.

"You can do this," says Scarlet. "Make me proud."

By using a brilliant disguise, the Minions sneak into the Tower of London, where the crown is kept. They work as a team, using Herb's evil gadgets along the way. Stuart hypnotizes the guards. Kevin blasts the door with his Lava-Lamp Gun.

"Topalino la crowna!" he says. The crown is in its case, right in front of them!

Bob uses his Stretch Suit to cut through the top of the metal case, opening it like a can opener. He reaches in, and his gloved hand grazes the crown's sparkly jewels. Only a few more inches, and Scarlet's heist will be complete! But just as Bob is about to wrap his fingers around the treasure, the crown starts moving. It's being taken to the queen!

The queen's guards are carrying the crown to her carriage. They place it on her head, and the carriage rolls down the street in front of a large crowd of people. Kevin, Stuart, and Bob's little Minion legs can't keep up—the crown is getting farther and farther away.

Then Bob gets an idea. He activates his Stretch Suit's legs. Suddenly, Bob is super tall! He takes off after the queen's carriage, passing all of London's famous sites. He grabs Kevin and Stuart and tosses them onto the carriage. A chase ensues!

Kevin tries to steer the carriage while Stuart attempts to snatch the crown from the queen's head. The carriage is out of control! Bob uses his Stretch Suit to save the carriage from falling into the River Thames, but he can't save it from crashing into a tree. *BOOM!*

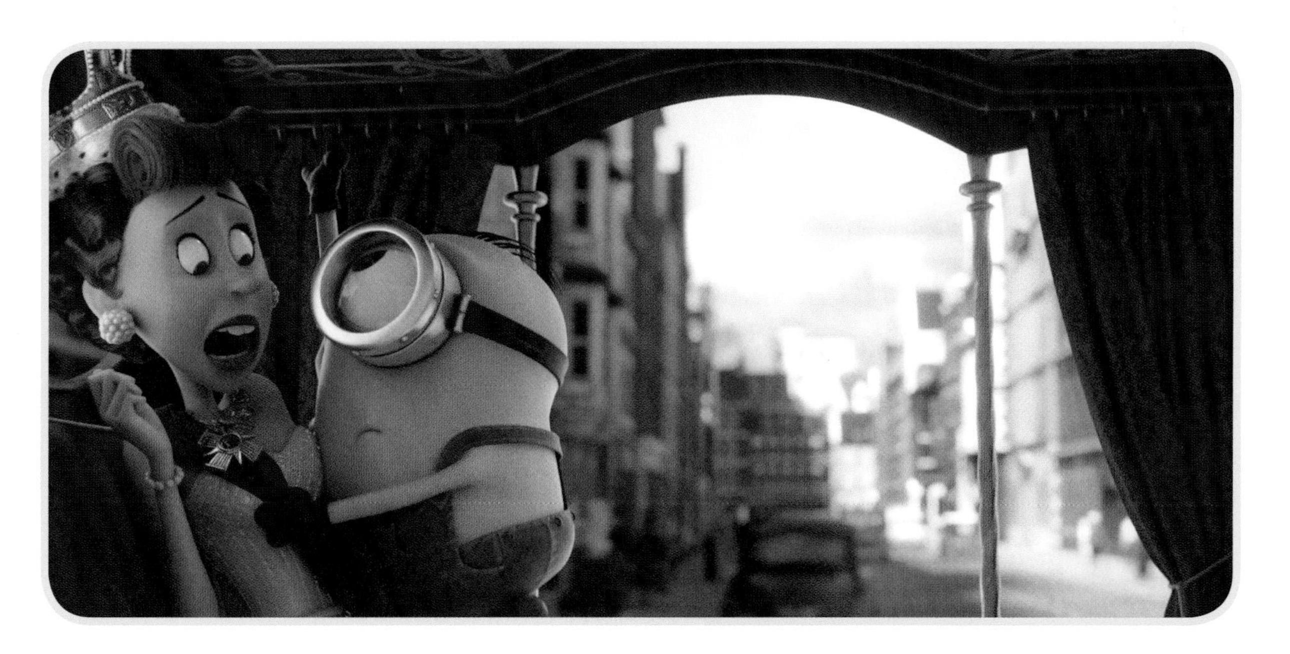

As the dust settles, Stuart grabs the crown from the queen. But policemen arrive and immediately chase after the Minions! They tackle Kevin and Stuart, but Bob keeps running.

Bob runs all the way to the Sword in the Stone! He grabs the sword's handle, hoping the sword will scare away the policemen. He doesn't know that, according to the sword's legend, only the one true king can pry it from the stone. Miraculously, he gives it a tug and pulls it loose!

The crowd gasps. Even the police officers are stunned!

"It can't be," a man exclaims. "The legend has been fulfilled! The one to remove the sword from the stone will be named England's leader. This bald yellow child is our new king!"

"YOUR MAJESTY!" everyone cries, dropping to one knee.

"Uh...scusa?" says Bob.

It’s true: Bob, sweet little Minion, henchman of Scarlet Overkill, is now the king of England. Instead of stealing the royal crown for Scarlet, Bob is now wearing it himself! He is escorted to his new palace home in a limousine with Kevin and Stuart by his side. A royal advisor opens the door.

“Hello, King Bob,” says the advisor. “Welcome to Buckingham Palace.”

Bob peeks out the window and sees rows and rows of guards in their official uniforms. Bob is intimidated. He gets an idea and makes a request.

A moment later, Bob steps out of his limousine. The guards are now all dressed in yellow and wearing denim overalls, just like Minions!

Bob sighs happily. "Aww, buddies! Buddies! Buddies!"

He gives each guard a hug.

BOB
FOREVER
BOB
FOREVER

It’s time for King Bob’s royal address.

Bob walks out onto an enormous balcony. Thousands of people are gathered below, waiting to hear their new leader’s wise and thoughtful words.

Bob looks around. He clears his throat. He blinks a few times, saying nothing.

"KING BOB!" he shouts at last. The crowd erupts in cheers.

"King Bob!" they cry. "King Bob! Woo-hoo!"

Bob delivers a long speech in Minionese, but the crowd looks on in confusion. So he shrugs and yells, "KING BOB!" The crowd goes wild again.

Back inside the palace, the Minions make themselves right at home. Bob slides down the banister of the grand staircase.

Kevin plays polo while riding a royal dog.
Stuart takes a long soak in the palace spa.

With so many fancy things to use and royal perks to enjoy, the Minions nearly forget all about Scarlet Overkill. But Scarlet hasn't forgotten about them.

One day, as Bob sits for his official royal portrait, Scarlet storms in.

"How dare you!" she yells, flushed with anger. "You stole my dream! I was going to conquer England someday! There was going to be a coronation, and I was going to be made QUEEN. Every moment was planned, I would wear a dress so sparkly it glowed, and EVERYONE WHO EVER DOUBTED ME would be watching, and they would be CRYING. I was going to be the picture of elegance and class, and you PINHEADS screwed it up!"

Bob feels terrible. He knows Scarlet is right: A Minion's job is to serve evildoers, not take over their plans. He removes the crown from his head and offers it to his boss.

"La crowna, para tu," he says.

"No, no, no, King Bob! You cannot just give up the throne!" says the royal advisor. "There are laws!"

"Laws?" says Bob. "Bob maka te laws."

In his final act as king, Bob heads to England's parliament to write a new rule: From this moment on, Scarlet Overkill will be England's new, evil queen.

Bob pounds his gavel. "La keena pota Scarlet Popapeil!" he says, presenting her with the royal crown.

“I don’t know what to say,” says Scarlet. “I just want to thank the Minions. I couldn’t have done it without them. Kevin, Bob, and Stuart, you have stolen not just England, but my heart.”

The reign of King Bob draws to a close. It is the shortest rule of any monarch in the history of the world. But Bob does not despair. He was a king for all of eight days, but he'll be a Minion for life. Bob, Kevin, and Stuart look forward to being Scarlet's henchmen again. And really, what could possibly go wrong?